Easter Bunny on the Loose!

By Wendy Wax

Illustrations by Dave Garbot

HARPER

An Imprint of HarperCollinsPublishers

The Suspects...

Emergency in Easterville! One of these suspects stole the Easter Bunny's Golden Egg! The Easter Bunny is on the lookout for clues that the egg-snatcher left behind. It's up to you to figure out who did it.

Fifi the Flower Fairy

Chuck the Chick

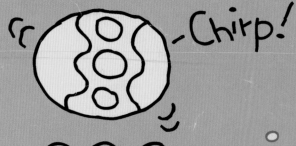

"-Chirp!"

Milo the Turtle

Find the clues hidden on each page to help the Easter Bunny catch the culprit. You must hurry. It's almost Easter, and there's no time to lose!

Kiki the Cuckoo

Duffy the Lamb

Gwen the Hen

Who took the Golden Egg?

The Easter Bunny finds something the egg-snatcher lost. It's your first clue! Find the Easter Bunny and see what he's holding.

Everyone at the Easter Factory is busy, busy, busy. *Aha!* The Easter Bunny has found another clue! What did the egg-snatcher leave behind?

The Easter Bunny hops through the crowded store—and guess what he finds. Another clue! Do you know what it is?

The Easter Bunny isn't looking for sweets or treats—he's looking for a clue! It doesn't take long for him to spot one. What has the Easter Bunny found?

Instead of stopping to smell the roses, the Easter Bunny zips right over to a clue. What did the egg-snatcher drop this time?

Out of the coop, through the barn, down to the pond, the Easter Bunny searches all over the farm for a clue. Just when he's about to give up, he finds one. What is it?

Bird-watching is fun, but finding the egg-snatcher is urgent! While searching among the leaves, the Easter Bunny comes across a clue! What is he holding?

Bonk! Bonk! The Easter Bunny dodges flying balls as he hops from game to game—but then he spies something the egg-snatcher left behind. Can you find the clue?

No time to color eggs with an egg-snatcher on the loose! The Easter Bunny searches his house, desperate to find a . . . There it is–another clue!

While everyone else is building floats for the Easter Parade, the Easter Bunny discovers a colorful clue. Do you know what he finds?

Tomorrow is the big Easter egg hunt! The Easter Bunny seeks one last clue—and he finds it! Now use your smarts to figure out who stole the Golden Egg.

Spotted Ribbon

Violet Flower

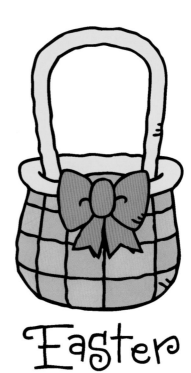

Easter Basket

Easter Bonnet

Jelly Beans

Green Shoe

Have you figured out who stole the Golden Egg? If not, look closely at the eleven clues and see which one of the suspects has all of them. Now do you know who the egg-snatcher is?

APR 2013

Pink

That's right! It's Fifi the Flower Fairy.
Fifi does the Easter Bunny's gardening.
She wanted to surprise the Easter Bunny by
planting the Golden Egg and growing a Golden
Egg Tree. It didn't quite work out as planned,
but she meant well.